BLOCK LEGEND PAPER
BY THE TON VII

KEVIN GREEN

authorHOUSE®

AuthorHouse™
1663 Liberty Drive
Bloomington, IN 47403
www.authorhouse.com
Phone: 833-262-8899

Published by AuthorHouse 11/16/2020

ISBN: 978-1-6655-0817-9 (sc)
ISBN: 978-1-6655-0816-2 (e)

I came from a parallel dimention to protect the light you see

I was picked up and devoured by giants that came to take this life you see.

I was caught standing across

Stained and brained as a product of torture,

Blooded, child abused and neglected.

Labeled the enforcer the unfortunate,

The lesser than as the stars fall

Scared by other

Smothered by others

Captured and slain

How many logs can a woodchuck chuck

How many beetles can the unfortunate fit on a string

Pain is thoughtless,

As I witness torture

And man slaughter reign

Supreme

Still haunted by the fright and sight of the bloodshed

That cools the pain

As I'm swallowed by the giants that come forth

Once upon a drafty night

I stared into the shadows through the mist

And saw a ghostly figure

Floating under the mid summers light

And I looked again,

But there was no one,

I looked again,

I tried to hold on to my potna and they all turned to ashes

I tried to call my friend but he turned to ashes

I knew I was tripping,

When the shadows I see didn't originate from me

My reflection,

Someone standing in the dark

Maybe a killer

Waiting for me

So high I almost feel like

Letting a blast of light

They though the whole to hate me

Threatening to kill me if I fuck around and fuck their bitches

Planning to kick in the door with the four

To kill me and take my shit

POEM

Somewhere between the lines of distant space, far from sight, right under your nose, not yet visible to you, where life is seen from a different point of view, where there is no instincts, and where everything is old and new, there is no hatred here, only just, and righteous, a place where life can renew again, not apart from life to sea, there are some that wish they could take something they consider life from me those who blame their triumphs, and downfalls on me, hidden in plain sight between the lines of life, imaginary to those who dare not believe in sight. The unknown will never know what I am or, believe in what I can become, those that fear what you consider death, without changing what life is, those so young at heart, interested in those who change life to art, becoming a creator of sorts, molding life with every stroke of the pen, changing life with every bush of canvas, those who notice the change of the color of the skin, mocking life, and time to maintain comfort for self, hidden in life, the cure for illness in health. Those to careless to care for self, only believing what one's eyes can see, there is a greater world behind the eye of the free from what you consider life after afterlife, creation where ideas are born and reborn to life, molding from the hands of the creator of life. There are closed channels from those with narrow minds, life left unseen by the eyes of mankind. Something too amazing for thoughts, much to comprehend, my life has no start, and life has no end, thought sent through space and time, to children so kind of heart, new life that begins to spark, where there's lines in life, man tends to arc. Life should have no end, now begin to start. The truth hidden between the lines of life, careful some villains have need action, life to some is more than satisfaction learn what life is and what life must become, on your journey there will be an end to so, between the lines of life, might contain a clue. You are partial to me, and I am all of you until the time that life learn farewell a due, until learn life anew.

ALTERNATIVE POEM

It is in my head, the meaning of life, madness engulfed by light, the sickening of lights and stage fright, the end of life, the end of light that mangles the sight. It is in the head, behind the third eye of lead, capable of capturing the thoughts in my head, catching blood of blue, bleed of red, oxygen toxifying the thoughts in my head. Why must I feel the pain of life raped in torment and torture the brain of Christ, feeling life to return light. It is in my head, the madness within, deeper than flesh and the pain within. It is in my head, I feel the pain over, and over again, release me now from this mental pain within, one deeper than life and pain. It's in my head over and over again. It is the reaper closing in, or is it the pain and torture that opt in. It's in my head over and over again. It's in my head life and light landed by light even in afterlight. I need the pain to see what is laying the hidden deep inside of me. It's in my head watching blood turn to bloodshed meeting the pain in my head, hidden deep within the third eye of life, pain is the rimmade to the light, and the afterlife. It's in my head, pain and blood shed, tainting the soul that line the messages in the head. It's in my head, the end of life, the end of light, the mingles the sight. (It's in my head.)

POEM

As frightful as life may become, one must never fear, for within the darkness. The light is here, never needing to fear the unknown, there is nothing but truth life, when one feels helpless in life, find truth in light, there is no fear, why fear the night. This is life with the absence of fright, bathed in the light, engulfed by light. There is nothing but truth in this unknown world of sight.

Life, creation from ones creator who attracted your mold of life, like stardust which in turn brought a new sun to life, like life which in turn brings fourth to light, unity in form is in turn a form of life, darkness is the true opposite of ones form of light, what once was dark shall now be brought to light, a perfect creation, of life to light in sight, if one can unveil the true meaning of the perfect creation of life, one will then turn, turn is known to be true to light, and bring what is unknown to life, like the sun above who in turn, bring forth the light, revealing in turn the true meaning to life, let what once was dark in turn, turn to light, and bring forth what is unknown to life, understanding the meaning to my life and the mold to life, what once was dark is now seen by light.

So much talent in the world,

sometimes it's hard to see,

a shining start like me

thankful for those who see

the better side of me

No more tears for those who lost love,

There has to be

More to life,

Than this constant push and shove,

Pouring out liquor for the stars above,

Here is heaven in a bottle from me with love,

I can never forget those I hold close,

I love much more than most,

These tears are for you,

Heart deeper than the ocean blue,

Baby this world's for you,

What once was can be a loving memory for you from me

Why can't you see me, invisible to the eye, look and there's no one there, detached from life like there's no one here. How could someone so close seem so far from touch. Never have I known the burning of lust to burn so much. This feeling is eating alive, someone unknown to me who doesn't notice I'm alive. Longing to understand life, and the beating of this man's heart, unseen my love and life, why do I feel like I've been divided in two, half of the stolen by the beauty of life that lies within her eyes, beautiful like the rain, beauty like the summers sunrise that seems so close, but remains so far from heart. Hello is but only a word from heart, but my life is still unseen, my exterior remain silent, but what about the life that lies between. Hello is not the word for me, invisible to life, misunderstood by beauty, braised by lust and one's imagination. Why is Hello a word too good for me. Mrs. Perfection, haven't seen the light that shines, like a Holy Man blinded by his beliefs on his shrine, such a beauty of life is never a waste of time, living on the warmth of beauty, could GOD make such beauty in life, she might be meant for mem detached from life, apart from me, missing me, how rare a privilege this beauty in sight, me half a man stricken by stage fright. Hello to you my Dear, as I am seen by light, a smile has seen me as life, releasing me from fear, letting thy should know, there is heaven here, such beauty in life, the answer for ones longing. I am but a man, flesh and bone. Forgive me Father for I have sinned shall I atom. Hello belongs to me, a brief conversation to some, but she is the world to me the life that life can now see. I would just like to let you know, you aren't invisible to me.

I must be out of my mind, these niggas don't got love for me, mix it, and twist it, I'm full blown, like the volume turned all the way up, on my microphone, like my last bitch I'm gone, think these bitches got love for me, I must be out of my mind, hustling, pushing game, toating grind. You think I'd let these niggas catch me slipping, you must have lost your mind, the feelings for my nine aint hard to find, toating this piece of mine, pushing your head back your piece of mine, fuck the penn, and jail time for crime. I'd rather squeeze the life out of a dime, and these niggas think you ain't supposed to go hard on a bitch, you must have lost your mind, I wouldn't give a bitch an inch. Slapping bitches on the ass, watching their ass twitch thinking your bitch ain't for me, you must be out of your mind. Bitch, tell her face, my dick is hard to find. These niggas ain't got love for me, It's all about the money, nigga it's all about the grind, gambling with this life of mine, like I lost my mind, I hear niggas hating that's why I toat my nine nigga, don't stand close to me, even when I'm highly intoxicated in the V.I.P. these niggas ain't nothing like me, these niggas don't out of town like me. You ain't the worlds most hated like me, that's why these niggas don't grind like me, sucka and sugar free. Spitting, writing, and dope dealing until they take my life from me. Here goes another clip just for not liking me, like I was Tina Turner and they were iking me, that just the hate in these niggas exciting me, I guess it's just the hard knock life in me, like standing in the court room, listening to the jury, lifting me, soon as I turn my back these niggas, knifing me, waiting to take my life from me, but real niggas got to eat, competing for turf on concrete, give me mine, hungry enough to squeeze a mill outta dime, blowing bomb in the air loving this life of mine, don't want a bill out of a crime, you must have lost your mind, these niggas hate, cause your grind ain't like mine cause you don't pistol toat to spine, I'm a Boss in the game, and you act like I lost my mind, for coming in town with Money and Dope shine, giving bitches Dope and Dope lives, fucking bitches on ecstasy, then fuck this bitches and bitch nigga standing next to me, forever sucka free, stuck to the grind like I'm supposed to be, remember these motherfuckers ain't got love for me, waiting and willing to put the knife in me, trusting these niggas ain't right for me. I'm too deep in the Hame I could be the life of me. I'm a Boss homie that's why you ain't liking me, hating me for writing me, but just like the penn you just another bitch nigga exciting me, fuck these bitch and bitch niggas not liking me. I'm game paid and Boss laid, bitch nigga How you liking me, you might just be another bitch talking shit exciting me, these are the do's and don'ts of this life of mine. The grift and the grind to this life of crime, double up on a nickle to dime, thinking I ain't about paper, like you lost your mind, rubberbanding G stacks a thousand at a time, all this from a strap, a pinch of snow, like a nickle and a dime got the whole block going cocaine crazy, like I lost your mind, with more than a brick to shine, assault rifle on deck, no more liking mine, they might hit your house, but they ain't hitting mine, deep in traffic riding with my hand on strap like I lost my mind. I'm more than a Boss, and a Dope line, cut to mix to cook, and watch the Dope shine, this is more than Boss to Hook to Dope lines. Now what do you know about dope and the dope grind.

Stars, Stripes, Bars and Scars. Bad Bitches and Sports Cars, like slim thug I'm the Boss, plus a brick to toss, have you ever made a nigga tongue kiss a glock, nigga you pussy, and I'm not, the weather man like Coke to Dope shot, me and my million dollar spot, my life's on me, so deep in the trenches I can't even trust the homie, I could never trust a nigga who owe me. Homie that what the game showed me, gripping my strap, too much money invested in the grind to turn back. I'm a Boss in the game, cause I earned that, reacting off the cognac, as the wheels turn, and blunts burn, watching time turn back, hoping these fake ass niggas aint the end of me, don't worry about me, I got my nine and my lawyer defending me. Until the end of me, soaking up all the hater these bitches send to me, don't hold your tongue you aint affending me, remember these niggas ain't as real as the pretend to be, but this aint pretend to me, sucka I'm realer than real, like a key in the field. My Dope so good you might catch a chill, remember it's real in the field, niggas die everyday, call it the battle field, I'm so cold, chilling on top cause my Game so old, talking bitches out they panties with this game told, and it's still money over bitches and stitche, you bitch niggas, and I'm soaking up Dope money like top notch figure. Holla at your homie when your pockets get bigger, I'm just a Boss taking liquor like to the liver. As I shot stand, and deliver, you know me. I stay sugar and sucka free, money in my hand cause it's C.O.D. these bitches ain't gone be the death of me. Shoot first and never ask shit, just cock back to blast it, blastard another head blown face down in a casket. I know you hate me, I chose the grit and grind fuck the VIP thse white bitches aint nothing but a double up to me, these niggas aint nothing but runner ups to me, a dope sac aint nothing but a bubble up tom, I hate to say it but I love these bitches sucking to me, and they are envious, but they aint knowing why we so quick to bust, living life with strips then the stretchmarks on my chest, leave a nigga white a whole in the head. God bless.

Have you ever seen a dragon spit fire, the pen is the only reason Dope dealers retire. Cooking to game like crack, you know how real niggas act, like face to face with a real nigga with a gat, I want all the dope in your pocket plus my money back, like the last boy scout I'm the quarter back running trapped, the end zone belongs to me, sitting on top of the world setting hands free, violate the violators ain't no time for haters. Deep on the grind you might like me now or later. Smoking that OG Kush, I'm so in love, with the bomb sailor, but it's the money I savor, I'm grit to the grind. One of the mind, turning pennies to dimes. Shining like a light, I shine and shine bright, got the whole world addicted to white, like the time when I write. I shine and shine bright, on the left and to the right, the nigga turn the day into night, cause my game is tight who else you know who can make a million dollars off a flight and more than what I write, I'm more than the birds that take flight. I'm the nigga to grind to life, and I'm no lie, turning bunds to ash, watching the smoke like limber in the sky. You should buy my dope high and shine cause I'm so fly. I'm too high to lie, in love with Dope money with a Dope high, duct tape and wrap up life, just to watch the Dope fly. Watching dope friends super man off a Dope high, hoping these niggas aint the end of me, reliever than you pretend to me, standing on top of the world until the feds send for me.

I do, what money do, and do not testify, why is it always the best die, I could change the world in a day, with niggas who collect dirty money and don't play. I am concrete like all dimes from block of yea, moving like turn tables move from my spot, cruising as I'm moving pushing my block. I can put a smile on your face like hip-hop. I'm about the release nigga you've seen today and money only make sense to you, I was told never give a bitch an inch. I started off with a pinch.

I could never lose it all. A Dope dealer like me meant to ball, sitting on racks and racks riding my Chevys like Cadilacs, moving flocks from left to right, this is the Dope Game a blessing to life, a 9 to 5 aint meant for me. I got a sac of some purp and a fifth and that's it for me, potent like bomb smoke, stay lit for me. Most of these niggas and bitches aint shit to me, as I ride like riders do, as youngsta I did not understand hate. But now I do, riding strapped hoping I ain't got to aim at you, another day, in the life like frosted flakes and your average coke price, this is just another slice of life, I'm just another player watching the sun come up, I've been grinding all night, and my pockets don't sleep, they hold cash and heat, this is the Dopeman show now find a seat. I bought the world for a day, without a realest, and took the dope game over without a peep, too much bullshit in the game, everbody selling their soul for the price of fame, I want the world in my pocket, no more suckas and sellouts on mine, just my fifth and my nine fit to spine, then I got the feds fucking with my mind, they almost robbed me blind and it's still over bitches on mine. I feel like I'm losing my mind, remembering my lost ones with this twist lime. If I have live without drug money I would have lost my mind. Like getting evicted for the third time. I guess nothing but the grind for me, but the hustle to me is like 1,2,3. I hustle before A B C, I'm back again, like rolling up another blunt. Smelling that weed in the wind, with nothing but money on my mind, counting my dollars making sure then in all one of kind. I love money, like I lost my mind, counting dope money in the sunshine, the bottom wasn't meant for me, my life is the realest then TV, homie I'm on the grind. Like dope to dope shot, like a Gee pinch to a dope knot, making dollars like a dope spot I'm the realest nigga I know, from the brim to toe, I push bomb and pimp hoe, they send two, and I send four, spitting game like the winds blow, up on stacks feeling 10'4" money was meant for me, like copyrights and royalties, and most of these bitches is flees and nigga I'm on the grind easing my mind, judging these felonies, popping my cooler where I go, right now, I'm fucking with nothing but shady niggas that's why I never call you back, mix it and twisted on this cogner but much love to my niggas from the bay to sac. I'll never knock the hustle my nigga to hold you back, and much love to my niggas addicted to duct tape and wrap, sky is the limit my nigga never let them hold you back, remembering how I made all this happen with game and a doughsha sac, stay true to you and never ever let them hold you back, can't duck with every nigga, niggas shady. I already told you that, I could tell you I'm a real nigga, but I bet you never heard of that, like putting your life on the line just to earn the scratch, Dope dealing with no cash back. What's the use of pulling out your nine if you don't last that, most of these niggas fake in the game, and I want my cash back.

How can I lose with a royal flush, I'm out of this world like purple Kush, running the game like George Bush, my potah and life, something like a pound to push, I wonder what life has store for me, hating these niggas loving to hate on me. I wonder how many niggas down to die with me, and how any niggas down to ride with me, beautiful like diamonds in the sky. Loving how weed and sky don't lie. Watching birdies fly till they die, always there when niggas out just to get high ballas of the year over here. Surrounded by cash with no fear, just me and my strap standing here. For something like the man of the year, ballas who ball from coast to coast out here. I want shrimp and lobster for the rest of the year, grabbing them hips, telling that ass to come here. Bitch I'm the man of the year, aint nothing but bosses an players outta here. Told my mom, I'm all about a dollar, and I cant come home. I got the Feds and undercovers tapping my phone, I remember when it only costed a dime to call home, and how I got badged. Some listening to my phone, wow is me, I'm the boss I'm supposed to be, ain't too much heaven in hell, out here putting bitches on like at tails, ever wonder what I would be like without illegal drug, born and raised around real niggas in the yea that toat Dope and real niggas don't snitch on, and don't tell, we Ho slang, shit in nigga free with hands and both thongs, pimping these nines like pimps who band, addicted to the Dope slang, just riding to the best nigga, it no than, balloon baby bought my own diamond ring, loving what money on everytime I hear the phone ring, sugar money ain't a thing, look at much cake you can bake, if you put your mind to it, me and my heavy hitters, the block who trap a lot, hopping from state went on syrup sandwiches, to lobster and steak, sucka free for like, fuck nigga and a snake, hungry and just ate. I flow where ever the money, the go from green to blow, fucking wish niggas who push crack, codme, and snow. Fucking with niggas addicted to heroin and blow, pain, and cash is all I know, fucking niggas, searching for heaven since birth, why doesn't the pain ever go away. If I had to, I'd pack my bags and leave today, all this weight of a niggas shoulders, makes a nigga colder, living this life as a street soldier, watching my game and cash get older. Nigga I told, I'm down to through them from the shoulder, watching these dollars add up drinking until I throw up, blasting these fools when they run up, million dollar figures, with straps and wrap sheets, I'm a hustler my nigga, engulfed by weed smoke, living with my finger on the trigger. I'm your million dollar nigga, and it ain't never over, a true funk town soldier, loving is my 45 fit to grip, and how extra clip, clip to hip, filling a safe fit for grip. Putting another blunt to lip, nowadays, it aint never hard to slip, on toes at all times. I'm the type of nigga to breakdown a bird to all dimes, living the high life, avoiding hard times, slanging Dope like I lost my mind, nigga this world is mind, nigga I'm one of a kind, wondering if I can make it in this rap game for real, when I usually stock knots, from snow blocks, to make a mill out a mole hill, momma said I won't kill. But I show will, a true hustla into his game called Skerill, I'm sharper than porcupine, and realer then a hundred dollar bill, a million dollars on the table before the million dollar deal. I'm a boss to heart, I mean a Boss for real now a days you only need a pinch to make a mill, like fine twenties when you break a bill, you fuckin ball till you fall homie but I'm a boss for real, I had everything I ever wanted before the rap deal.

A million miles and running, got these niggas gunning for me strapped to the T waiting for these niggas waiting for me ain't no tears no more, just gun smoke and bomb weed floating out the window. I'm a boss baby and don't forget it. I'm strapped up down and with it, riding with a life sentence in the trunk, riding back to back with pump. It's time to dump, how aim and cock the pump. How many niggas down to ride with me, I'm pumped up, ready to blast the first to hit, 100 thousand for everybody I hit. I'm the shit, so fuck them niggas and everybody they fuck with, fuck you I'm the shit. The type of nigga that real niggas ride with, waiting for my piece of the pie, and this world is my fit, loading the chamber to spit down with everything you down with, most of these that's why cock back and blast my nine to spit. I'm gunning a million miles and running, tell me what you want from me, playboy, I'm coming.

A Hustla by nature

Never by choice

And I can make

A million dollas

Using my voice

And I can make

A million dollas

Using my voice

Walking on Dust and

Fully automatic busting

Don't mind me

That's just my automatic fussing

This is why I love me, you see

Yes, I love me, you see

Can't nobody else love me, like me

Because I love me, you see

And this is why I love me, you see

Yes, I love me you see

Yes, I love me you see

Feeling alone,

And separate from life,

Surrounded by a sea of people,

Tell me Lord

Why do the winds

Deceive me

I don't understand

How something so beautiful,

Such as a woman,

Can take the life

Of a MAN.

I hope for Happiness,

So why do they wish me Hell

A man between life and death,

I wonder where will this life take me

Ain't nigga alive I feel more

Stomping and pimping in my steel toes pushing pussy like fillmore. 68 to 69 now she 87, dead in the window, pimping like slim from Fillmore. Still pimping in in my steel toe, pushing million dollar hits that the Dope friends feel more, this is the real shit, that real niggas kill for, all for respect and the love for BIG Dough, fuck these haters as I spill flow, watching dope friends, kill snow I'm a true Boss for real, like 43 off steel, a true Boss for real like a Billion Dollar deal, look but don't touch, I love to bust so much a true Boss such, as I mash the gas and pop the clutch, with a throw away too hot to touch, these haters is the reason why fake niggas die so much

I've been treated like a slave my whole life, I'm the block hustling my life who's to tell. Who's wrong and who's aint. Strapped to the teeth cause, nowadays niggas don't have time to, it can all come to an end with a fresh flash, knowing how niggas don't care about life, I blast first ain't got time to fight, on the block hustling gambling my life no winners we all lose. Strung up like guitar strings in the out of blues, I'm a real nigga, I ain't time to lose, you snooze to lose, I win homie because I choose, stuck to life like rhythm, timeless and priceless like a true dime, I was told you would live your life to shine stunting a piece and a piece of ???. I aint going nowhere and these niggas ain't taking mine. Shooting first these niggas ain't taking my, you must be losing your mind. I'm a boss player, I aint wasting time, you thought I lost my mind, like a Boss and these niggas aint taking mine, My life is like 40 days and 40 nights of rain, Dope money spends the same, with bomb on my brain its hard to maintain like a dick to the brain, am I insane or not, strapped up the Dope spot, beamed and bomed out, stacking crazy loot lookback and aim to shoot. Love my life, my life won't look same, hunted and hated like police when they aim shoot, wow is me, finally I'm the Boss I'm suppose to be, cutting honors like cake, still one of them niggas you love to hate. Niggas testing my nuts, that's why I cockback to bust, like niggas to love to luff, it's nothing to me, strap to spin chopping a Chapter key, these niggas should know better then to fuck with me, I'm completely, the G I'm the supposed to be a Hustla by future, counting Dope money cause the Dope came has choosing, standing a Billion strong off clean cut and a bitchy, nigga don't bother me.

Riding high ass fuck beating round date block, and the police ain't shit, mine to spine without an extra clip, time is money and I'm all about stacking a gangsta grip, hustla by nature never by choice, it ain't nothing but the grind I swear, niggas try to test my nut sac but I test them niggas that don't dare, riding high like need in the air I swear, me my nut sac and my pistol glare, like a pistol player like toes tip to air, I'm a motherfucking playa with my pistol. I wonder what life would be like if I pimp the air, me my bomb sac and grip to snear, hot as fuck like I pimped the mayor, get in when I fit in like clip to ear, cash rules everything around me nigga listen near, real estate investing like hear, most of these nigga hate like a simp fear, hundred thousand dollar loan, nigga listen hear, none of yall niggas niggas could be us, killas and Dope dealers that we trust and these are the moss bergs, and glocks trust. Those ain't niggas alive that we trust, trapped by the magic, caught in the web of life, up and downs like the Dope game and the coke price. Why is criminal action and federal entrapment overhead, like a Dope house full of bread, I'm a Boss baby and you ain't hear a word. I said, throw a pinch in the game with some elbow grease now I'm flying in and out of state two or three times a week, niggas federally contagious, be cautious of who you touch, 5 to 10 plus a finger on the trigga and I trust no nigga. I'm riding high, have you watching blunts die, and thugs cry.

I've seem bomb multiply, probation plus a Dope sac and strap of them niggas to put the town on the map, I'm the game lord, pimp slap, living with my pistol on my lap, the hustle, the grind in this life of mine, where two dollars is a 4 of a kind. The time is money, so stop wasting mine, I'm squeezing the life out of nigga, you only need a pinch to shine, bomb keeping more money on my mind. Going back to Cali to blaze up or the sunshine, homie this world is mine, me and my bro to spine, loving this California grind, time is money so stop wasting mine. Fuck what you say this world is mine. Enemy of the State eating mash potatps and milk, on probation jumping from state to state, got cocaine, finishing from plate to plate. I'm too real to except the fake, well and raised around niggas who's friend to take. Killas and the dealers who triple to shake, with more chicken to make. God I love money, there's so much money to take. Busting on all these bitches who scream to take, niggas high, no lie. Using my nine as an alibi, real niggas, we all lie. Like nigga don't die and bitch they multiply and to all my real niggas rest in peace. I'll be on call until it's time to release the beast. I cockback and blast on these niggas before they release the beast. I've got a glock gave you can't beat, I've been fucking bitches strap since sesame street, first you cockback to aim and blaze the heat, now turn the boss up and blaze the ride with strap on lap, fuck under the seat, I'm a boss baby, with the cock price you can't beat, if you don't grind you don't eat.

POEM

Death in the midst of sadness, burned by sorrow, only to live again, tortured by the chill and the madness of the wind, non-existing by twilight with no ending in sight. Trapped by the pattern of life, where does the pain end, sicken by the houles that blow in the wind. Death sounds so sweet, the ending of pain and the beginning of peace. I shall no more be haunted by the beast, hearing the winds call on me, peace shall come soon, with no end to me, still in person, as the rains enter me, the chills and pains of the life, that winds sent to me, no sounds, no light, no clear of day to take away, the sadness of day, ever so still, hoping to blow away, take me away, the winds I say. Away from all this madness and this sickening of life. Is it only death do I receive paradise, impatient for afterlife of life, there must be a cure to what ills me. Here is the midst of death and sadness cover from my head to toe, in what man calls madness. If only I could fly away. Leaving to stay Death disarray, confused by life and life's dismay. Should one be reborn? Just to live life unwhole again, returning like the rains, replaying this life of pain, in love with sorrow, so comforting and home, here to live and die, alone, feeling the near and nearer than life, holding on to life preparing for the afterlife, no more pain shall come, here today, gone tomorrow as the rains come, here and gone. I am me in a mourn, not to blame life so soon, with only sadness, and madness to offer, the price for living, cursed until death takes me away. Free from now on, as the chill carries away. There must be more to live for, feeling the beauty of the drum from beneath the earth's core, sadness and dismay tempting as ever, here today and gone tomorrow like the flight of a feather, life forever, changing like the winds and weather changing like the seasons come and go, remembering life as loving love song, here today, gone tomorrow as life moves on, non existing by twilight, sickened by sight, sinking forever deeper in the midst of light.

YESTERDAY

I cant understand why my love wasn't good enough for you, embedded in the dark awaiting what waits for you, tell me why isn't love good enough for you. Drunken sadness lurks within my beating heart not knowing when to end and when to start, is this empty love I feel burning in my heart, loves not good enough, feed up with your lies, sorry I've had enough, my love's not good enough, can you explain what went wrong, was it the sadness that trapped you so far away, from this love song, here today gone tomorrow that's all I have to say. No more madness, sorry, love's gone away, she brought her heart back here yesterday, no more pain, sorry it's gone away, love hurts me deeply that's all I have to say, remembering when my love wasn't good enough for you, broken hearted, crying over you, now knowing what to do. I was so in love with you. Now, it's all over and this is the end for you, sorry my heart wasn't good enough for you, for the empty bottles, and lust that broke in two. Sorry that my love isn't good enough for you. This is the sadness, wrapped in the madness, I was here patiently waiting for you, sorry love's over and this is the end of you, here today gone tomorrow that's all I have to say for you. No more lies, sorry my life's gone astray, that's all I have to say. She brought her back here yesterday, no more pain here in my heart, sorry I've gone away, your love hurts deeply there's nothing left to say, here today, gone tomorrow, so what happened to my yesterday?

POEM

What happen to tomorrow, there goes my yesterday, drunkening the madness, no love here to stay, smothered by sadness, there goes my yesterday hello to tomorrow, and goodbye to yesterday, my love gone astray, now goodbye to yesterday.

Life under fire, living life as a live wine, who won test me its to the end of my friend. Should I remain in darkness or be seen by light, stuck in the warzone with niggas that gunfight, duck and cover my niggas as my bullets take flight, my 45 can turn your day to night, money, murder and mayhem is all that niggas talk, money breeds jealousy watching bullshit walk. Watching bitches soak up game that real niggas talk, you wouldn't believe the lines I walked, life outlined in calk, duct tape and wrapping that money I walk, fake nigga squilk and bitch up, and real niggas don't talk, walking out the court room with the high priced lamery I bought, money breeds envy, but that bitch nigga just aint me, cursed by life when will the hate end, just a real nigga born in this world of sin, trying to avoid the pen, life tatted on pad by pen, hated by life cause of this world I'm in cursed by sin. I know you hate me, but its just another day under fire as a live wire, strapped and pushed ya, hustling 24 hours a day, nigga snitch that's why I trust nobody, just me and my girlfriend and my moss berg shottie, game, related simple and plain, deep in the trenches doing the damn thang. Caught up in the warzone where niggas cock back and I'm, but to me, my nigga it's just an everyday thing. Sliding around the block letting my nuts swing, where niggas ride dirty, and slang kang, trust nobody we all in it for the same thing. Who won, test me, in the for the loot so fuck thy enemy, the grind is the cure and the remedy, duct tape and wrapping everything then send to me, life under fire, explosive like a live mind, in love with money and murder, it's all about cocaine so fuck what you heard of, nigga bleed jealousy and spit murder. Sicker than the next nigga, and harder than you've ever heard of. Life under fire, when the pistol start to pop there's no need to cease fire, outlined in calk. Money makes cents so let that bullshit walk, real niggas don't speak, we slang Dope and gun talk.

POEM

God, greater than man, the words of mankind. The creator of the son. Here before so called life and death, something much more than man. What thy eye can see, greater than the moon, the sands of time, the wind and sea, possible to contain the uncontainable image of the one, the creator of creation of the one who hold the sun, through me, might hear a story of life. Find the good book and learn the teachings of Christ, learning how life puts and ending to life, learning how the past, present can show you the future of life. To me, personally is more than just the meaning of life, much more than wisdom and the known gift of sight, darker than darkness, and the gift to life. The loving one, who gave the gift to life, caring for forgotten soul sweep the afterlife. The one who must know all, the one who taught the stars, and the rains to fall, watching the world cry for me it seems. But something life feels just like a Dream. The owner of the world it seems. The bringer of wishes and wonder dreams, wonder if man can truly understand the meaning of life of true man of earth, wind, water, fire and ice, understanding. There is not death to life, the walker of different dimensions, the teacher to fire, and ice, the one to fourth energy to Death to life, to me peace and immortality the meaning to life, testing souls who dream to become the creator of life. Why must life continue to feed from is praying for more meaning to life, slapped in the face by the many prayers to life. Why must one continue to need more than the living to life. Why must one continue to need more than the living to life. Greed followed by envy, jealousy and sin by blowing softly in the wind. Wiseman say seek and thy shall find, the answers to life and forgiveness of time. If one of the ability to be free, than in time. One will truly see me, and much more than man, and the words of mankind. The creator of man, the earth, time, and mankind.

POEM

Watching the reflection in the mist of the mourning dew, waiting to be born again. Soaking the earth in mourn again, wet and yet still thirsting for life, a mirror image of life and paradise, another tear of GOD, life feeding on sadness, dew reflecting a perfect picture of life, and the colors of rain. Here today gone tomorrow to e once more born again. Finding meaning to this so called meaningless life here once again comes the beginning, the end to life, all under the heavenly sky. Breathing in the moisture of the wind, under the falling sky reflecting the chill of the wind. Watching the clouds cry, how could I be, a reflection of life, weathering away, here today gone tomorrow. To live another day, born under the stars, and moon, a reflection of life watching the earth bloom. So beautiful life has become, a reflection of life, living under the sun, the moon, the earth and sun working as one. What would life become without one another, what would life be without the birth of father and mother, loving birth, life, father and thy mother. Giving hope, love and thankfulness to thy loving brother, a reflection of life and love from thy loving mother. Watching life's reflection, in the light of day as day becomes night, and night becomes day, life is all one in the same, a reflection of life in mourning dew, once again born again, tears of rain, reflection of life, watching life be born again.

Take the life of mine and I am left with something you cannot see, a temple of life, nothing but a mold of me. Breaking free amazed by life and its hold on me. Cosmic dust creating your mold of life, answers embedded in your mold life for eternal life; do what they will, contain the secrets of life waiting break free, seen in the light afraid of the dark side of me, this mold life, this life of me, attraction under the sun like lige to sunshine, with can be overcome, if the will is strong enough, time to reveal and until the secrets of life, Keys to unlock life and life's afterlife, some in the end of creation, when each thought has been foresee, the real meaning of life, and what lies between confusion and obstacle to reality and the truth of life, imprisoned by fear, and ignorance of the unknown section of life, and the great untold, what lies within the truth of mold, life of mine with so much truth untold, is life to you contain by you, life something more, it is true ignorance to say life is only ensure life is nothing more, foresee what is and will be it is life to this life from me, light educating this life of me, with holding to truth to is seen understanding life to light and what lies between revealing the light and to some unseen, unknown numbers of life, and light yet seen, visions tell the ____ of life yet seen, immortality and peace of life to reveal the light seen, restricted lite, lies and lust, and the truth of life unseen he who refuses to help life shall be blinded light, and secrets unknown being fourth restriction of life and life untold, poisoning the light destroying life that light brings, confusions will tell the tales of stories that unseen, destructions is not what should be, another obstacle of life, and what life light could be, progress is the key to open many unknown door of light, creations of ones or fit to mold you tight, first was darkness, then was light, just like the night in turns to light life giving from creation from ones creator fit to mold you right, there was darkness which in turn brings forth the gifts of life, immortality lies seen the fine lines of life, if one is willing to reveal what has been seen in light, to life which can be brought to light, secrets withheld in dark which in turn burned to light, unity is needed to nurture the seed to faith the destroyed of most, bringing the end of life for the sake of religion when the truth is so far from heart. Scapegoats for life who is to blame, blaming life and limb, blaming the night, and dim blaming the words of him, blaming life for the life you took from him. How righteous thou must be, to be cleaned of conscience like he. Even in the end of me, you will never have the right of me, when the days come short to release the light in me how can one believe in the existence of life and limb, and say you own the right of him. He who sacrificed his life and limb, cold faces of so called faith in this life of grim, to do it all again they would still take the life of him, because of the sacrifice of his life and him, would one so bold of faith, sacrifice your life for him, or watch death and dismay as they stone and turn life to dim, I can never say I am as right as him, but life, is it those who wish for his piece of life calls for peace of life, it is those who wish for his piece of life those who speak of truth and faith, those who choose to pick of fate to give and take. I am not the one to judge fate or the faithful, just living life so sweet and tasteful, giving thanks to those who remain truly grateful, blessed like those who remain truly faithful, whatever happen to love thy brother, tales of tales from man, son from mother to brother, will to will and let thy love thy mother, withheld from the fight between thy brother, life let thy love thy mother, withheld from the fight between thy brother, life I was told was righteous and living, as life feeds off life, leaving the faithful praying and hoping for afterlife, condemning life from death because of fear and fright, putting the fear of GOD in thy heart because ever life dies in the light room for the righteous and religion, forever grateful for what is life and living, what do I see, faith a destroyer of life, so called righteous life praying for the afterlife. I'm not the one to judge your right. I'm just a watcher observing the light.

POEM

Dying day after day, sitting with this hole in my heart, without you watching my world fall apart. Putting together the pieces of a broken heart, this is the end. And I do not know where to start, she gone again, how can I go on living without my only friend, picking up the wild roses blessed by your touch. How could I let go the one I love so much. Remembering the sweet rains and the tender warmth of her touch. Dying day after day, remembering the day I let my heart slip away. The woman that touched my heart, how do I mend this shattered and broken heart, trying to catch memories of the past. Where do I start, watching the sand in the hourglass, my love to pass. This time, this love won't last, there's too much pain that remains, inside this broken heart of min. They say all mortal wounds heal in time, no longer blinded by this love of mine. Watching my world fall apart, I just don't know how and where to start. Dying day after day, sitting with this hole in my heart. How could I lose my only friend, remembering her dancing in the wind, she's gone again. And then the rain comes, tears from a broken heart, putting together the pieces of this broken heart.

I once met a man who loved to share, he believe that woman are meant for only an instant like a breath of fresh air. Lasting only a moment in time, thinking if only this woman was mine. Man please woman life before the beginning of time. Only with a loving friend could I ever share this life of mine. But only for a moment in time, only if this woman was mine.

POEM

Life like food to the soul, forever existing, tight holds on life like water and air, in and out of life, like a faithful prayer. Layers of thoughts within and upon me, thirsting for knowledgement fit for the soul. Now holding in my hands the key to life, longing for a life fir for life. Immortalize by the knowledge that lie within. Beauty deeper than thy own skin, soaking in the beauty of life, amazing in all ways. Like the moon light, that shines at the end of the days. Always to return again. Like life to whom to pale ski. Braised by the light, mortality the food of life. Existing but for only a minute of time. I stand the same as humankind, bleeding beautifully like a wonderfully aged wine. Wise men say life become sweeter with time, is there ever enough time after this life of me. Blessed thou are with every meal and glass of wine, blessed thou are for becoming part of time, life, food for the soul. Engulfed by light as faith unfolds. Beauty like the reddest rose, hiding in secret stories yet untold. Fate is forsaken, listening to the stories wise man told, grateful are the old and wise, blessed by day to witness the sunrise witty in life. Talking in the winds wondering about the beauties in life, one does not always wait the afterlife, to witness paradise. All one has to do is take hold the beauty of life, food for the soul, the water watching the beauty of life unfold.

POEM

Stories of life brought here to sight, stories of dark seen by bit. Stories of men, some great, some sin and spite, men smothered day seen by light, here lie tails of life. Should one chain in the dark or become seen by light. I've once seen a man eager to sight, and eye sore to some. But there's always a meaning to it, looked and frowned upon as a frown to life, what lies in the dark always seen in light. No ordinary man just frowned upon by life, no ordinary man, a man whose words brought meaning to life, trampled by public, stubborn in life. No one to listen a man who has seen the life, a man with words and the meaning to be, a man who has been through it all, from dark and brought forth meaning to light. But who wants to listen to man less than by life. I heard the man say that seen the end would come. I've seen it all, and this will be the end of some. Then I hear the man say, I have seen the light. Even the dark is seem by the light, protect your wines and your children. By the scene of night, for wickedness and destruction foreseen by light. But the one lookers wouldn't believe in life, belief for a beggar with esteem for life. Laughing at a man who has seen the light. For I say, I've seen the end, and it's the end to come. Old man you must have lost your soul in a battle of all. As the clouds started to roll in, watching the rain pour down and close in, watching him consume life, as the waters begin to shower, nah sayers gathering the children as the village people scatter. I've never seen a rain with such power. Sweeping life away with a blink of an eye, watching life running from the sky, washed away by the waters and the winds, stories of life, with life seen again. Ordinary man of sight, this man who has seen the light, smothered day seen by light, no ordinary man in this tail of life. What lies in the dark is seen by light, these stories of men, some great, some of sin, and spite. What lie in the dark is seen by light. Only wise man head the warnings of Life.

I picked this collection of songs and poems to inspire the world with my expression and view of life from my point of view. I started writing these pieces of art many years ago when I was surrounded by hater in a great time of need. I had to take a journey inside myself and create my own happiness and these songs, poems, and information poured out through a pen, helping me in a great time of need. I wanted to share with you the reader this collection of ideas, hoping to entertain and tickle the imagination of the world. The creation of this collection was a great step in the right direction in a great time of need. I am pleased with the outcome of this collection and hope to bring greater understanding peace, love, happiness and entertainment to you the reader in this great journey called life.